HELLO NEIGHBORS

Written by
Sarah Toast

Cover illustrated by
Eddie Young

Interior illustrated by
Joe Veno

Louis Weber, C.E.O.
Publications International, Ltd.
7373 North Cicero Avenue
Lincolnwood, Illinois 60646

Manufactured in U.S.A.

8 7 6 5 4 3 2 1

ISBN: 0-7853-1068-1

This is the most exciting day of Danny's life. His mom and dad just bought him a brand-new bicycle. It is shiny and red and has training wheels, which help Danny stay balanced while he learns to ride his first bicycle.

"Go ahead and ride around the block, Danny. We will be right behind you if you need help," says his mom. Danny pushes off and starts to pedal down the sidewalk.

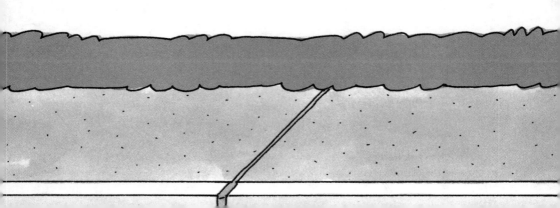

Danny sees the mailman up ahead. He zooms past to show how fast he can go on his new bike. "Hello!" says Danny.

"Whoa!" says the mailman. "That's a fast bike you've got there! Are you the Pony Express?"

Danny is careful not to knock over the trash cans the garbage collector is emptying. "Hello!" says Danny.

"I'll trade you a can of trash for that bike," laughs the garbage collector as Danny speeds by.

Danny pulls into the gas station on the corner. He wants to show his new bike to Bill who works there. Danny rides over the cord that makes a bell ring inside the station. *Bump, bump* goes his bicycle. *Ding, ding* goes the gas station bell.

Bill walks outside to see who his customer is.

"Hello!" says Danny.

"Hello, Danny! That's a fine bicycle you're riding. How about some air in those new tires?" asks Bill. He shows Danny how to use the air hose and sends him on his way.

"Thanks, Bill!" calls Danny.

Danny rides past the neighborhood grocery store. "Hello!" says Danny.

The grocer says, "Your bike is as shiny and red as my apples. Catch!" He tosses an apple to Danny. Danny thanks him and keeps pedaling.

Danny slows down at the next corner of his block. A police officer is there directing traffic and helping people cross the street. Danny knows he is not supposed to cross the busy street, but he likes to see the police officer at work. He stops and says, "Hello!"

"Look both ways before crossing the street on that new bike," says the police officer.

"I'm not crossing the street today. I'm just going around the block to show my new bike to my neighborhood friends," says Danny.

"Thanks for stopping to say hello," says the police officer.

Danny pedals past his neighbor who has a pretty flower garden in her yard. "Hello!" says Danny.

"That new bike is as pretty as a rose," smiles the lady as she waters her flowers. She accidentally waters Danny, too.

Danny rides past the firehouse just in time to see the firefighters pull up in the fire truck. "Hello!" says Danny.

"You're going so fast you could be going to a fire!" they say.

Danny is almost home when he rides past people working in the street. "Hello!" says Danny.

"Nice wheels, kid!" says one of the friendly workers.

"Take good care of your bike," says the other worker.

"I will!" promises Danny as he rides on.

When Danny gets home he sees his best friend, Ralph. Ralph has a new bike, too. "Let's go around the block so you can show your new bike to the neighbors," says Danny. And that's just what they do.